For my father,
John Tucker –
good on the bongos.
E.G.

First published in North America in 2019 by Boxer Books Limited.
www.boxerbooks.com
Boxer® is a registered trademark of Boxer Books Limited.
Text and illustrations copyright © 2019 Emma Garcia
The right of Emma Garcia to be identified as the author and illustrator
of this work has been asserted by her in accordance with the Copyright,
Designs and Patents Act, 1988.
Library of Congress Cataloging-in-Publication Data available.
The illustrations were prepared using hand-printed paper and acrylic paints.
The text is set in American Typewriter.

ISBN 978-1-910716-36-6

1 3 5 7 9 10 8 6 4 2
Printed in China

All of our papers are sourced from managed forests and renewable resources.

Plinka Plinka Shake Shake

Emma Garcia

Boxer Books

What's in the music box?

Let's have a look.

A **ukulele** . . .

Plinka

Plinka

shake

shake

and **maracas**.

Triangle . . .

Ting

Ting

Ting

and **cymbals**.

Bongos . . .

pata pata

and **kazoos.**

A **whistle** . . .

Peep

peep

Bash

and a **tambourine**.

Claves . . .

ToK

ToK

ToK

and **chime bars.**

Tinkle Tinkle

Castanets . . .

Click
Clack

and a **drum**.

Güiro . . .

Chacka

Chacka

Chacka

and **bells.**

Jingle Jangle

Agogo . . .

Ding

Dong

and **xylophone**.

Shhh now,
stop playing.

Quiet in the room.

Look at all these **instruments**.

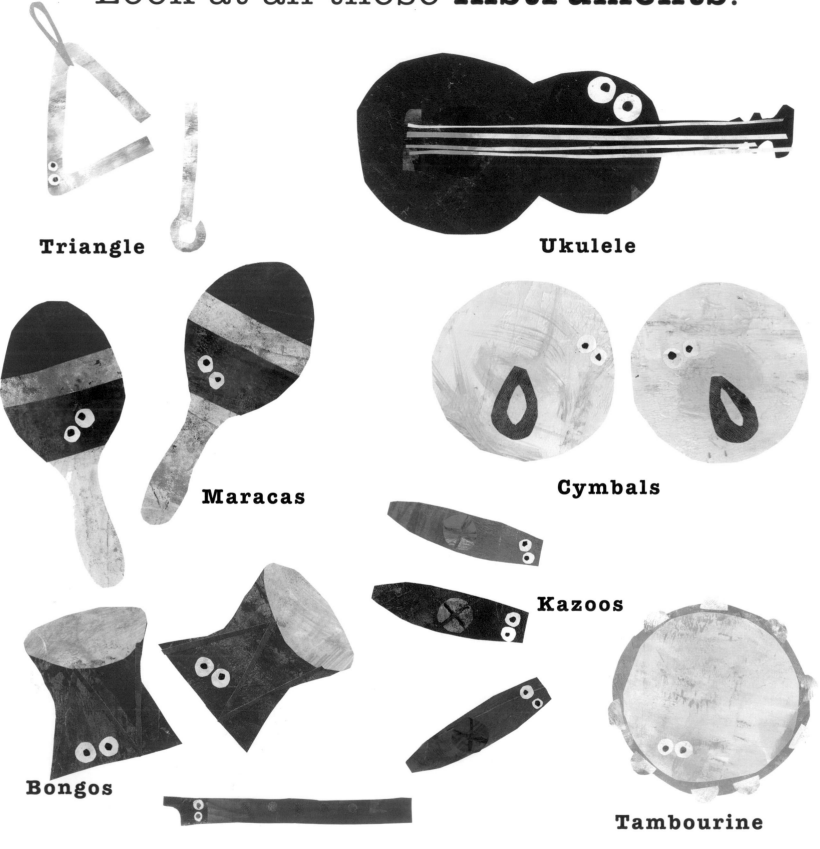

Triangle

Ukulele

Maracas

Cymbals

Kazoos

Bongos

Whistle

Tambourine

Shall we play a **tune**?

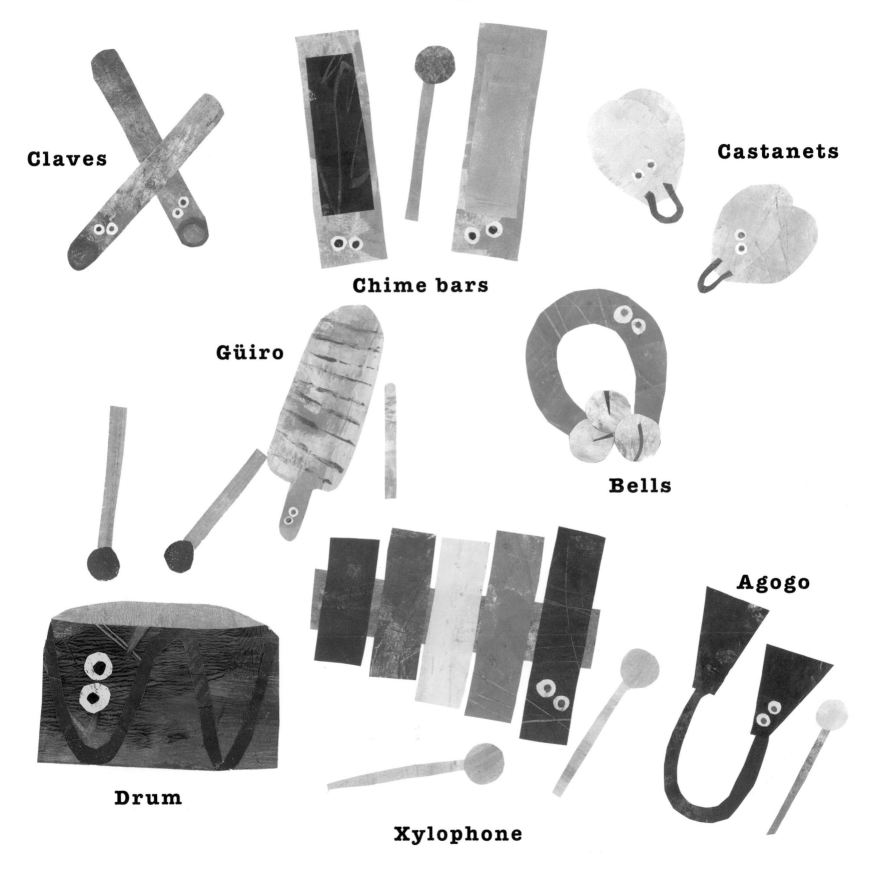

Claves

Chime bars

Castanets

Güiro

Bells

Agogo

Drum

Xylophone

Plinka Plinka
Shake Shake
Ting Ting
Crash
Pata Pata
Wha Woo
Peep Peep
Bash

Once more from the top.

Tok Tok
Tinkle Tinkle
Click Clack
Boom
Chaka Chaka
Jingle Jangle
Ding Dong
Zoom

Let's play another **tune**!